"You never know your luck."

In the mouse shed, Charlie selected a handsome blue buck and a pretty cream doe (as yellowish a cream as he could find) and put them in a cage together. He thought of telephoning Merry to tell her what he'd done, but then decided against it.

"One thing's certain," he said to the potbellied pig at lunchtime. "Their babies will be blue or they'll be cream, or maybe some will be a creamy blue and some a bluish cream. But a green mouse! As impossible as a green pig! Or a green cow or a green horse. It's only birds and fish and reptiles that are green, not mammals. Ridiculous idea!"

Also by Dick King-Smith:

For older readers:

Charlie Muffin's Miracle Mouse

DICK KING-SMITH

Illustrated by Lina Chesak

A KNOPF PAPERBACK
ALFRED A. KNOPF
NEW YORK

A KNOPF PAPERBACK PUBLISHED BY ALFRED A. KNOPF

Text copyright © 1998 by Fox Busters, Ltd.
Illustrations copyright © 1999 by Lina Chesak
Cover art copyright © 1999 by Lina Chesak

www.randomhouse.com/kids

Library of Congress Cataloging-in-Publication Data
King-Smith, Dick.
Charlie muffin's miracle mouse / Dick King-Smith ; illustrated by Lina
Chesak.
p.   cm.
Summary: After many unsuccessful attempts, lonely mouse farmer Charlie
Muffin finally breeds a green mouse, finds true love, and wins the Best of
Show at the Grand Mouse Championship Show.
[1. Mice—Fiction.] I. Chesak, Lina, ill.   II. Title.
PZ7.K5892Ho   1999
[Fic]—dc21   98-37961

ISBN 0-517-80033-0 (trade)
ISBN 0-517-80034-9 (lib. bdg.)
ISBN 0-375-81007-2 (pbk.)

First Knopf Paperback edition: November 2000
Printed in the United States of America
10 9 8 7 6 5 4 3 2 1

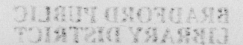

Contents

Chapter 1

The Mouse Shed

Mr. Muffin was a very special sort of farmer. We all know that there are dairy farmers and sheep farmers and pig farmers and poultry farmers. But Mr. Muffin was a mouse farmer.

He was a breeder of every imaginable color of pet mouse, and he kept hundreds and hundreds of them in a big shed. That was really all his farm was—just a big shed, around the sides of which were rows and rows of little cages, stacked on top of each other from floor to ceiling. And on the front of this shed was a large sign that read:

MUFFIN'S HIGH-CLASS MICE

Another animal that Mr. Muffin kept on his mouse farm was a large dog, the largest you can possibly imagine, which stood in the mouth of its doghouse near the door of the mouse shed. On the doghouse was another sign. This one read:

CAVE CANEM
(PLEASE NOTE:
THIS IS LATIN FOR
BEWARE OF THE DOG)

The animal always stood there, day in, day out, because it was, in fact, a stuffed dog.

For as well as being a mouse farmer, Mr. Muffin was a very clever do-it-yourself man who understood all about electrical and mechanical gadgets and gizmos of every kind.

Inside the stuffed dog, he had fitted an electric motor that was activated each time anyone walked toward the door of the mouse shed. Then the dog's great jaws would open and shut, while from deep inside it came fierce barks and thunderous growls, enough to frighten away any mouse burglar.

Mr. Muffin was very proud of his guard dog, which, of course, barked and growled at him every time he went to attend to his mice. He would pat the top of its huge head and say, "Good old Major!" (For this had been its name in life.)

Major stood sentry outside the mouse shed, but inside there was still a need to guard against thieves, for the food that Mr. Muffin fed to his pet mice was attractive to wild mice too. To discourage these from coming into the shed, he kept within it two cats and an owl—all, of course, stuffed.

As a boy, Mr. Muffin had liked model trains, and now he put his hobby to good use. A little train track ran around the four sides of the floor of the shed, carrying supplies to the pet mice. At the doorway it passed through a tunnel, which Mr. Muffin had to step over when he came into the shed.

There were four model locomotives, each pulling a string of freight cars, to help the mouse farmer in his daily chores. One train carried birdseed (the principal food of the mice), one carried clean water for their drinking bottles, and one carried fresh sawdust. The fourth train started each journey with empty cars, which would then be filled with the dirty bedding from the floors of the cages.

Within this outer oblong railway system was a second, circular track, around which the two cats, each mounted on its own wheels, moved endlessly, day and night. One was a black cat with white paws, and one was a tabby. And at intervals there came from their wide-open, sharp-toothed mouths harsh meows to frighten away any wild mouse that might venture in.

The pet mice, born and bred in the shed, took no notice of the cats, nor of the owl, which was suspended with ever-spread wings from another electrically powered contrivance in the roof and which glided ceaselessly above the cats with mournful hoots.

Imagine the scene as Mr. Muffin comes in every morning to tend his high-class mice.

First, as he approaches, Major begins to growl and bark. Mr. Muffin pats him and speaks to him. Then he opens the mouse-shed door, to be greeted by the usual chorus of meows and hoots. He steps over the tunnel and makes his way to the far end of

the building, where the four model loco-motives are waiting, in their own shed.

Using a hand-operated remote control, Mr. Muffin presses a button to start up the first locomotive. Under his direction it moves out onto the turntable, which is then rotated so that it can reverse into a siding where a line of empty cars is wait-ing. The four trains are known as the Food Train, the Water Train, the Sawdust Train, and the Dirty Train.

The first one to start the day's work is the Dirty Train, and once the locomotive is coupled to its cars, Mr. Muffin directs it out, across a set of switches and onto the main line, stopping at each tier of mouse cages and loading the cars with damp, mucky mouse-poo.

Once the Dirty Train has made its circuit of the shed, the Sawdust Train is started up to go through the same procedure, followed in turn by the Water Train and the Food Train.

Then, when all the pet mice have been cleaned out and watered and fed, Mr. Muffin shuts the door upon the mournful chorus of cats and owl and, to the sound of Major's barking, goes to get his own breakfast.

Later, there will be customers coming to the mouse farm to buy pet mice. There may also be customers needing Mr. Muffin's services as a taxidermist, bringing with them their beloved dead pets to be stuffed, so that they never need be parted from them.

There is a third class of person who may visit Mr. Muffin's mouse farm, in addition to those who wish to buy live mice or to have a pet stuffed. For sometimes, no matter how well and carefully he looks after them, a few of Mr. Muffin's mice die. "Waste not, want not" is a motto of his, and the third class of person comes because they know that Mr. Muffin, mouse farmer and taxidermist, sells not only live mice, but stuffed ones too.

"No trouble," he says to such a customer, "no smell, no feeding needed, and they'll look ever so pretty on your mantelpiece."

Chapter 2

Merry

Indeed, on his own mantelpiece, in the living room of the farmhouse, there were several stuffed mice of various colors, as well as other creatures that he had found dead and had not wanted to waste—a squirrel, a toad, a hedgehog, and a number of small birds.

As a taxidermist, Mr. Muffin was willing to have a go at preserving any sort of animal, no matter how large (he had, in fact, done a pretty good job with a Jersey cow and with several ponies), but generally he preferred to deal with the smaller ones; they were more of a challenge.

Sometimes his customers were not quite satisfied with the results of the taxidermist's work on their dear departed pets ("Well, it's not really a good likeness, he was never as fat as that," or "She was always so happy, but you've made her look a bit miserable"). In such cases, Mr. Muffin did not charge for the work done but kept the stuffed animal instead, so that his house gradually became filled with silent, motionless figures. There was a potbellied pig in the kitchen, and in various other rooms there stood pet rabbits and guinea pigs and even a rather moth-eaten monkey, while in his own bedroom a parrot perched on the end of the bed, regarding him un-blinkingly with straw-colored glass eyes.

Mr. Muffin was particularly proud of the display in the bathroom, where he could lie back in the warm bathwater and look up at the big glass tank that hung sus-pended from the ceiling. In it there floated three large stuffed goldfish that he had fitted with artificial swim bladders, so that they never rose to the surface or sank to the bottom, but hung forever motionless above his head.

One downstairs room in the farmhouse was used as the taxidermist's workshop. In it there were always a number of dead ani-mals, some in the process of being stuffed and mounted, some waiting their turn in the large freezer.

Here Mr. Muffin would work happily away upon his subjects (mostly dogs—they were the most common), unless he heard his own dog barking to announce someone's arrival. Then he would go out, to find the person looking rather nervous—for Major was quite a frightening sight—and he would pat the great beast's head and say, "Quiet, boy, quiet," whereupon Major would fall silent (for his owner had pressed a small switch behind his ear that turned off the mechanism), and Mr. Muffin would lead the way into the mouse shed, or into the workshop, as the case might be.

Twice a day, of course, every day of the

FRAGILE

year, Christmas Day and all, taxidermy was forgotten as the mouse farmer attended to his hundreds of live pets. Mr. Muffin could never take a vacation, because for an hour or so each morning and again each evening there were the four trains to be run—the Dirty, the Sawdust, the Water, and the Food Trains.

But he did not mind the work. On the one hand, he was happy in his workshop, perhaps putting the finishing touches on a sloppy-looking old spaniel sitting, gazing adoringly upward ("We want him to be waiting for his biscuit, like he always did"), or a cat curled in a sleeping position ("We're going to put her near the fire, where she always lay"). On the other hand, he loved to leave his mouse shed, on his way to breakfast or to supper, knowing that every cage was clean, every one of his many-colored pets fed and watered.

And what a variety of colors he kept! People coming to buy their child a pet from Muffin's High-Class Mice had such a selection from which to choose.

There were white mice with pink eyes, and white mice with black eyes, there were cream mice and fawn mice and deep auburn red and slate-blue and chocolate and piebald mice, and there were others whose smooth coats were known by such attractive names as "dove" or "champagne." And as well, Mr. Muffin bred long-haired mice and curly-coated mice—though these were, of course, more expensive. The pink-eyed white mice were the cheapest, and the mouse farmer sold more of these, but all the other colors were very popular with children, and during the summer months and especially the school vacations the taxidermy would be often interrupted by Major's warning.

But then one fine August day, something happened that was to change Mr. Muffin's entire life.

He was in his workshop, fitting a pair of glass eyes on a bony old greyhound, when he heard his guard dog barking.

He gave the greyhound a pat.

"Don't move," he said, and went out to the mouse shed, only to find that there was no one to be seen and that the door of the shed was wide open.

Mouse burglars! thought Mr. Muffin. I must have forgotten to lock the door when I came in for breakfast. He ran back into his workshop.

Here on the wall was a control panel, specially designed to deal with such emergencies, and now he began to press switches to put into action Operation Mousetrap. One switch closed and locked the mouse-shed door, a second halted and silenced the two cats and the owl, and a third operated an intercom. Into this, Mr. Muffin now spoke.

"You are under citizen's arrest," he said in a stern voice, "and are warned against touching the tracks, locomotives, or rolling stock, which are electrified. Remain quite still until the arrival of the police."

Then he pressed a fourth switch on the control panel: this activated a closed-circuit television system. Looking into the monitor, expecting to see an ugly gang of thieves stealing his precious mice, he saw instead the solitary figure of a young woman— and a rather nice-looking young woman, at that.

Mr. Muffin had never had much to do with young women. For one thing, he'd been far too busy with his mice and with his taxidermy to have time for any kind of social life. For another, he'd always been rather shy with the opposite sex. If ever he thought about marriage, he just couldn't imagine any woman wanting to live in a house filled with stuffed creatures, and a freezer full of dead ones. And as for the mice, why, women were scared stiff of mice—everyone knew that.

But this one didn't seem to be, for as

Mr. Muffin watched, she stepped carefully over the railroad tracks and peered with interest into the nearest cages.

Mr. Muffin began to feel a little foolish. Operation Mousetrap seemed to have been a bit over the top. Pausing only to press a fifth switch—to unlock the door—he made his way out, silencing Major as he passed, and entered the mouse shed.

"Good morning," he said gruffly.

The young woman turned around.

"Oh, hello," she said. "Are you the police?"

"No," he said. "My name is Muffin."

"Oh, look, Mr. Muffin," the young woman said, "I'm awfully sorry, but the door wasn't locked so I'm afraid I just walked in."

She smiled, and Mr. Muffin thought what a nice smile it was, and what a nice face she had.

"Didn't my dog frighten you?" he asked.

She laughed.

"No," she said, "but whoever stuffed him has done a marvelous job of it. And he barks and growls beautifully."

Mr. Muffin felt a glow of pleasure at these words, but still tried to keep his voice stern as he said, "Perhaps you wouldn't mind telling me who you are and what you want?"

"My name," said the young woman, "is Merry Day. And I want to buy a high-class mouse, please."

Chapter 3

No Such Word as *Can't*

"For a child?" asked the mouse farmer.

"No, for me," said Merry Day. "I always wanted a pet mouse when I was a little girl, but my parents said, 'No. Mice smell.' These don't seem to."

"The bucks do, a bit," said Mr. Muffin. "So, if you want one mouse, you should get a doe"—he shot a glance at her left hand and saw that the fingers were ringless— "Miss Day."

"Call me Merry."

"Oh. Right ho," said Mr. Muffin.

Strangely, he didn't feel the usual shyness. Strangely, he was glad the fingers were ringless.

"My name's Charlie," he said.

"Can I call you that?"

"Oh. Yes. Of course."

"Well, then, Charlie," said Merry as naturally as if she'd known him for ages, "you'd better advise me what mouse to buy. I live on my own, you see—I've got a little apartment—and my mouse will be company for me."

"Yes," said Charlie Muffin, "but really you'd do better to buy two mice. They'd be company for each other."

"But then there'd be lots of babies."

"Not if you had two does."

"That's what I'll do, then," said Merry. "But, oh, goodness, what colors shall I choose? You've got so many different ones, all so pretty.

"In fact," she said as they walked around the cages, "you seem to have every possible color of mouse. Except green."

The mouse farmer burst out laughing.

"There's no such thing as a green mouse!" he said.

"You mean, no one has ever bred one before?"

"They couldn't. It can't be done."

"Charlie," said Merry. "I've got an old aunt who always says, 'There's no such word in the dictionary as *can't*.' You've bred all these lovely different shades of pet mice—like this amber-colored one, what is it called?"

"Champagne."

"And these coal black ones here, and these pretty blue ones. If you can breed blue mice, why not green ones?"

Mr. Muffin shook his head, smiling.

"If I could breed a green mouse," he said, "I'd be in the *Guinness Book of World Records*. I'd win the Supreme Championship at the Grand Mouse Championship Show. I'd be the most famous mouse fancier in the world. A green mouse! Talk about flying pigs! Now, then, come along, let's choose you a nice pair of young does. What color do you like?"

"Oh, sorry," said Merry. "I'm taking up your time."

But, in fact, it turned out that she took up the whole morning, so curious was she, first about the mice, then about the meowing cats and the hooting owl, and then about the trains, which she was allowed to run. And that led to Mr. Muffin inviting her into the house and making coffee for them both in the kitchen, which they drank, watched by the potbellied pig, and then showing her around his workshop, where the still-blind old greyhound stood patiently waiting for his new eyes.

So easy was Mr. Muffin in the company of his new friend that as they reentered the mouse shed, he actually showed her how to operate his guard dog.

"Scratch him behind his ear," he said, and she did so.

"There's some sort of switch here," she said.

"Press it," he said, and she did so, and Major began to bark and growl.

"How clever you are, Charlie," said Merry, "with all your gadgets, and your stuffed animals, and your mice. Choose two of them for me now, please."

"What colors?"

"I can't make up my mind."

"There's no such word in the dictionary as *can't*," said Charlie Muffin, grinning.

In the end Merry chose two of the prettiest of Muffin's High-Class Mice, a blue and a champagne, and bought some food to feed to them, and a cage to keep them in (for all of which, though she

didn't know it, Mr. Muffin only charged her half-price).

At the door of the shed they shook hands, while Major bellowed in their ears until the mouse farmer switched him off again.

"Good-bye, Charlie," said Merry, "and thank you so much. I've had such a lovely morning."

So have I, thought Charlie.

"One thing I'm sure of," she said.

"What's that?"

"If anyone ever succeeds in breeding a green mouse, it'll be you."

Charlie laughed.

"Good-bye, Merry," he said. "If you need any advice or anything, give me a ring," and then suddenly, even as he said those last four words while holding her right hand, he looked at her left and thought how much he would like to give her a ring, on that third finger.

Chapter 4

Mix Blue and Yellow

So dazed was Charlie Muffin by the events of the morning that he sat eating his lunch of cold ham and salad quite unaware that when he thought he was helping himself to chutney, it was actually marmalade. His mouth was full of meat, but his mind was full of Merry.

After lunch he went back to work on the greyhound, which ended up with one brown eye and one blue one. And for the rest of the day—and in the days to come—he dashed out, from workshop or mouse shed, whenever Major barked, hoping that it was not just any old customer but a special one.

After a week had gone by, Mr. Muffin discussed the matter with the parrot. As many lonely people do, he talked to his pets a good deal. The difference was that he talked to the dead ones as well as the living.

"Polly," he said, "I'm a stupid old fool."

The parrot did not comment.

"Here am I," he went on, "going all moony and spoony over a young woman I've only known a couple of hours. I can't stop thinking about her, but I'll bet you a pound of parrot seed she's never given me another thought. I'm right, aren't I?"

Of course, it may have been caused by Mr. Muffin getting out of bed at this point, but the parrot seemed to shake its head.

Later, as he was loading the Food Train, his phone in the mouse shed rang.

"Hello?" he said.

"Hello, Charlie. It's Merry. What are you doing?"

"Feeding the mice," said Charlie Muffin. And feeling very happy to hear your voice again, he thought.

"I've just fed mine."

"Are they all right?"

"Fine. Look, Charlie, I've been thinking. Did you ever do any painting—watercolors, I mean, at school, perhaps?"

"Yes."

"Well, do you remember what you get if you mix blue and yellow?"

"Yes. Green."

"Well, I know you haven't got any mice that are actually yellow, but those cream ones—they're yellowish, like the cream on Jersey milk. And you've certainly got blue mice. Try crossing a blue with a cream. You never know your luck."

Charlie's mouth was open, ready to say what a ridiculous idea this was, but then he heard a click as Merry hung up.

"Cross a blue with a cream, indeed!" he said to the cats as they trundled by.

"Meow! Meow!" they replied.

"All you'd get would be some blue cubs and some cream cubs," he said to the owl as it glided past above him.

"Hoo-hoo! Hoo-hoo!" it answered.

For the rest of that day, the mouse farmer thought about this preposterous idea. In fact, he thought about it so much that he made a silly mistake in his work as a taxidermist.

He had taken a rabbit and a guinea pig from the freezer. Working late to complete them, after making the evening round in the mouse shed, he went to bed that night quite unaware that the stuffed rabbit was now tailless, while on the stuffed guinea pig's bottom was a fluffy white cottontail.

Nonetheless, when he woke the next morning, he echoed Merry's words as he said to the parrot, "You never know your luck." And later, in the mouse shed, he selected a handsome blue buck and a pretty cream doe (as yellowish a cream as he could find) and put them in a cage together. He thought of telephoning Merry to tell her what he'd done, but then decided against it.

"Better to wait for five weeks or so," he said to the cream doe. "Three for your babies to be born, and then another couple of weeks for them to grow their coats and show their color."

"And one thing's certain," he said to the potbellied pig at lunchtime. "They'll be blue or they'll be cream, or maybe some will be a creamy blue and some a bluish cream. But a green mouse! As impossible as a green pig! Or a green cow or a green horse. It's only birds and fish and reptiles that are green, not mammals. Ridiculous idea!"

But when he went upstairs to bed that

night, there was the moth-eaten monkey hanging by one long arm from the banister, and when for once he looked carefully at it, he could see that it was indeed a monkey of a greenish color.

That night Charlie Muffin dreamed that time had moved magically on, and that the offspring of the creamy yellow doe and the blue buck had been born and had grown their coats and that every single one of them was as green as the young spring grass.

But, in reality, it wasn't like that at all.

When the time did come, the cubs were colored just as he'd told the pig they would be. Not one of them had even a single green hair.

During all this time, Mr. Muffin had

neither seen nor heard anything of Merry Day.

"She's forgotten about me, I expect," he said to Major.

"Ruff! Ruff!" said the dog.

But then one morning when the Blue X Cream cubs were about six weeks old, Major began barking and then, before his owner had even left the workshop, stopped again.

Only one person knows how to switch him off, Charlie thought. And he ran out, and there was Merry. She looked very tan.

"Hello, Charlie," she said. "Sorry I haven't seen you for so long. I've been on vacation with a friend."

A *boyfriend,* thought Charlie Muffin. He couldn't remember ever having been jealous before, except perhaps of some breeder whose mice had been judged better than his own. But now a wave of jealousy washed over him.

"A friend?" he said in a thick voice.

"Yes, a girlfriend from the office."

"Oh," said Charlie. "Oh…um…did you have a nice time?"

"Very nice, though I worried a bit about Antonia and Cleopatra."

"Antonia and Cleopatra?"

"My mice. But another girlfriend looked after them beautifully for me, and they seemed very glad to have me back."

As am I, thought Charlie.

"You look well," he said.

"You look tired, Charlie," said Merry. "You've been working too hard, I expect.

I don't know how you manage. Couldn't you get someone to help you?"

I could, thought Charlie Muffin. A very special someone, if only she'd have me.

He took a deep breath.

"Merry," he said, and then he stopped.

"Yes?" she said.

"Oh, nothing."

Chapter 5

Color-feeding

"Did you think any more about what I suggested?" asked Merry. "About crossing a blue mouse with a yellowy cream one, I mean?"

"Yes," said the mouse farmer. "I did."

"And did you do anything about it?"

"Yes. The cubs are six weeks old now. And before you ask—no, none of them is the slightest bit green. I don't care what your old aunt says about 'No such thing as *can't.*' It *can't* be done."

"Charlie," said Merry. "My old aunt has lots of favorite sayings, and another is 'If at first you don't succeed, try, try again.' Please, may I see those babies?"

Mr. Muffin opened the door of the cage in which the cubs were, and Merry looked into the nest.

"They're so pretty," she said.

"But they're not green," Charlie said.

"You'd have been rather surprised if any of them had been, first try, wouldn't you?"

"I certainly would."

"Well, I don't know anything about breeding mice," said Merry, "but I'd have thought it always takes time to produce a brand-new color."

"It does. The only way is line breeding."

"What does that mean?"

"Well, for example, you'd have to cross a whole lot of bucks of one color with a whole lot of does of the other color. And then when their children were old enough, you'd mate them together, and so on, for perhaps five generations. Then you'd be breeding from the great-great-great-grandchildren of the original cubs. And all the time you'd be selecting the ones that were nearest in looks to whatever you were trying to finish up with—the biggest, or the slenderest, or the ones with the longest tails, or the spottiest."

"Or the greenest?" said Merry.

"Well, yes, strictly speaking. But I mean, look at this bunch, Merry. Not a green hair on any of them."

"No. But they might have green genes," said Merry.

She picked up one of the cubs.

"Just think," she said. "Your great-great-great-grandchild might be the world's first green mouse. If only Mr. Muffin here would try again."

Charlie Muffin sighed.

"Are you really telling me," he said, "that you want me to set up a complete line-breeding program, crossing blues and creams—"

"Custardy creams."

"What? Oh, all right—custardy creams, generation after generation? I know mice are quick breeders, but it could take a year before we see any results. Which we won't, because—"

"Don't say it, don't say it, Charlie," interrupted Merry. "Just think about another of my old aunt's sayings: 'Nothing ventured, nothing gained.'"

"I don't see why I *have* to venture," said Charlie.

"Don't you?" said Merry.

She looked into his eyes and smiled.

"It depends," she said, "on what you want to gain."

"What did she mean by that?" said Charlie to the parrot as he lay in bed that night. "Could she have meant that if I succeeded in breeding a green mouse, she would"—he stopped while the parrot stared blankly at him out of its straw-colored glass eyes—"marry me?" Charlie finished.

Of course, it may have been because he stretched his legs out before turning on his side, ready for sleep, but it did seem to him that the parrot nodded its head.

There's only one way to find out what she meant, he thought as he drifted off, and that's to do what she wants.

So the next morning, once he had started the Dirty Train on its circuit, he made a note, as he went along, of the cage numbers of six of the bluest of the blue bucks and six of the custardiest of the cream does. Later, he paired them all off, and then he found a large (green) notebook. On the cover he wrote:

BLUE X CREAM
LINE-BREEDING PROGRAM

and added the date. Then he entered the details of the six newly paired couples.

"I'm going to do this properly," he said to the cats as they trundled past, meowing. "This group will have babies in three weeks, and then another couple of months later those babies will be old enough to breed from, and so it will go on for five generations. By which time"—he said to the owl as it glided over his head—"we'll have a better idea of whether it's ever going to be born."

"Hoo–hoo! Hoo–hoo!" said the owl.

"Why, the green mouse, of course. Who did you think I meant, flatface?"

So the weeks passed and the seasons changed, and every couple of months or so a new generation of Blue X Cream mice was born and (once they'd grown their coats) eagerly examined for any trace of greenness.

So wrapped up in this experiment was Charlie Muffin that the standard of his work as a taxidermist dropped off a bit, and room had to be found in the farmhouse for a number of fresh substandard specimens. The owners of a dear departed Manx cat were less than pleased to find that Mr. Muffin had absently put a tail on their Tibby, while a nanny goat ended up with a pair of cow's horns, and a pet chicken with webbed feet.

All the time that the program went on,

Merry would come regularly—once every couple of weeks or so—to the mouse farm, to see what progress Charlie had made.

Every now and then he would be on the verge of asking her a particular question, but always his courage failed him at the last moment. It was a pity that Merry's old aunt wasn't around, for she would have said, "Faint heart never won fair lady."

But then there came a day when the

fair lady had a bright idea. She and Charlie were inspecting the latest litter of Blue X Cream babies—still not a green hair to be seen—and afterward she stayed on a little to watch Charlie working the four trains on the evening's cleaning, watering, and feeding routine.

When the Food Train drew up beside her, she said, "Don't you ever feed them anything besides birdseed?"

"Yes," said Charlie. "Sometimes. Stale bread, oats, bits of dog biscuit."

"No plant food? Grass, clover, dandelion, that sort of thing?"

"Small amounts, sometimes. Not too much—it would upset their stomachs. Why?"

"Well, I was looking at all those little cars

loaded with birdseed, and I suddenly remembered my grandfather's canaries."

"What about them?"

"He used to color-feed them."

"Color-feed?"

"Yes. He used to feed them egg food—hard-boiled egg chopped up very small (I was allowed to help him do that)—and then he'd mix it with a kind of sweet red pepper (it came from Spain, I seem to remember), and after a while this mixture actually began to alter the color of the bird, so that yellow canaries changed their coats to rich orange. Now, if we were to try color-feeding—feeding all those babies on green stuff, not too much, like you said, but more and more as their digestions got used to it—don't you think that might help to do the trick?"

Charlie smiled.

"No, Merry," he said. "I don't."

"Load of rubbish," he said to Major after she had gone.

"Ruff! Ruff!"

"Color-feeding, indeed! Just because it works for canaries!"

But all the same, there was an entry in the notebook that day that read:

> Began feeding small amounts of green stuff to the experimental stock. Groundsel (for minerals), dock leaves (antiseptic), clover (for the nervous system), chickweed (easily digestible), dandelion (good for the blood).

His day's work finished, Charlie came
into the house, hung his hat on one of the
cow horns of the nanny goat that now
stood by the front door, and went into the
kitchen to prepare his supper.

"Color-feeding," he said again, this
time to the potbellied pig. "You never
know, though, do you?"

The pig stared expressionlessly at him.

"It just *might* make the difference, I

suppose. What with my line breeding and now this idea of Merry's, maybe we're one step closer to the day when I'll be able to show the world Charlie Muffin's miracle mouse."

Chapter 6

Cage 87B

For quite a long while after that, Mr. Muffin was very busy in his workshop. He didn't for one moment forget his mice, of course. The Dirty, the Sawdust, the Water, and the Food Trains each made their twice-daily circuit, the cats meowed, the owl hooted, Major barked and growled.

As their numbers increased, more and more of the experimental stock in the line-breeding program were born and, once old enough, were now being fed quite large quantities of green stuff without harm. Bluish they were, and creamish—but greenish, no.

The mouse farmer examined each new litter carefully, though perhaps with not as much excitement now. But as a taxidermist he *was* very excited, because he was spending every minute he could spare to work on the biggest stuffed animal he'd ever done.

The zoo had asked him to prepare it for exhibition at the Natural History Museum. It was a giraffe.

Charlie Muffin realized straightaway the problems involved in stuffing a fifteen-foot-tall bull giraffe in a room with a twelve-foot-high ceiling. He could work, with the help of a stepladder, on the body and the legs all right, but what about the neck and head?

"I could have them sticking out of the window, I suppose," he said to the web-footed chicken, which stood by his workbench, "but they'd get wet when it rained, and, anyway, how would I ever get the whole animal out the window when it was finished?"

He sat looking at the workshop doors, which were double ones, plenty wide enough to let something like a hippopotamus through but not a fifteen-foot-high giraffe. Then, as he stood up, his sleeve brushed against the web-footed chicken, and it fell on its side.

"That's it!" shouted Charlie Muffin. "I'll do the body and legs standing up in here, and then, when that's finished, I'll lay it on its side. I can do the head and neck separately and stick them on afterward!"

As he was setting the chicken upright again on its webbed feet, he heard Major bark and then stop as he was switched off. So he knew it was Merry.

He ran out to see her in the doorway of the mouse shed.

"Merry! Merry!" he shouted. "I've got it!"

Merry's face lit up. Oh, Charlie, she thought, you clever man! No one's ever bred a mouse of that color before!

"Where is it?" she cried.

"Where is it?" said Charlie. "In my

workshop, of course. I couldn't think how to manage with such a tall animal, but now I have!" And he told her his plans for the dead giraffe. (It had been a matter of urgency to deal with it immediately, for giraffes don't fit inside freezers.)

"Clever, eh?" he said.

"Very," said Merry. "But can we go and look at the latest litter of Blue-by-Cream cubs?"

"You look at them," said Charlie. "I can't now. I must get the giraffe's hooves fitted. But I'd be glad if you had a look. I'm not sure if I have lately—I don't seem to have found the time."

"Which cage are they in?"

"Can't exactly remember. Number 87B, I think. It's written down in the notebook."

"Where's that?"

"I left it on top of the locomotive shed, if I remember rightly," said Charlie, and he hurried back to his workshop.

Merry went into the mouse shed, stepped over the tunnel, and made her way down to the far end. Oh, dear! she said to herself. Just for a moment I thought he'd done it. Maybe my old aunt's wrong, and *can't* is in the dictionary, after all.

On the flat top of the locomotive shed was the notebook and beside it the hand-operated remote control, which Charlie had taught her how to use.

With it she first switched off the cats and the owl, and then she chose one of the four locomotives, started it up, backed it up onto the turntable, directed it down the siding and out onto the main line, and then stood watching as it rattled around the track.

Without the weight of a string of loaded cars, it raced along, paintwork shining. On its side, in tiny gold lettering, was its name (THE FOOD), and above that the name of the line, MMMR (Muffin's Miniature Mouse Railroad).

"He's like a little boy, really," she said out loud. "I just wish..." and then she stopped and sighed again.

Once she had steered the Food back into the shed and lined it up beside the Water, the Sawdust, and the Dirty, she picked up the green-covered notebook.

First she looked at the page marked DIET, and saw that Charlie was now indeed feeding quite large quantities of green stuff to the experimental stock. Then she turned to BIRTHS and saw that the latest cubs to be born were, indeed, in cage 87B, and that they were already two weeks old.

They'll have grown their coats, then, thought Merry, and it seems as though Charlie hasn't inspected them lately. She found the right cage and opened the door.

Typically, Mr. Muffin had designed and built beautiful little nest boxes for his pregnant does to have their babies in. Besides having a round hole in the front through which the mother went in and out, each box had a sliding roof.

As the doe (a really custardy-cream one, Merry could see) came out of the hole, whiskers twitching, alert for food, Merry slid back the lid of the nest box. Gently, she teased open the nesting materials. With interest, but without any real hope, she peered in.

Then her eyes widened and her hand went to her throat and her mouth fell open, while from it came a strangled gasp.

In the workshop, Charlie Muffin was carefully fitting one of the great split hooves of the giraffe onto its pastern joint when the big double doors burst open and Merry came rushing in.

"Charlie!" she cried. "I've just looked in 87B! There're six of them, and five are blues, but quite a greenish sort of blue."

Charlie put down the hoof and stood up.

"What about the sixth one?" he said very quietly.

"It's green, Charlie, it's green! It's as green as a garden pea! Oh, Charlie!"

"Oh, Merry!" said Charlie, and he opened his arms wide and she rushed into them.

Chapter 7

Adam

Each still had an arm around the other as they stood before cage 87B and looked into the nest box. Very carefully, Charlie reached in, took out the green baby and, holding it by the root of its tail, examined its underbelly.

"It's a buck," he said.

"Is that a good thing or a bad thing?" asked Merry.

"Good. Once he's old enough, I can mate him with any number of different does—greenish ones, we hope, like the rest of these are—and, who knows, I may breed lots of green mice."

"*We* may breed lots of green mice," Merry said.

"D'you mean form a partnership? Muffin and Day, mouse farmers?"

"No, not Muffin and Day. Muffin and Muffin."

Again very carefully, Charlie put the green cub back with his brothers and sisters.

"Merry," he said slowly. "Are you saying that you will marry me?"

"I might, Charlie," said Merry. "If you ask me properly."

Down on his knees went Charlie Muffin beside the shining metal tracks of the MMMR. He reached for Merry's hand.

"Will you be my wife?" he asked.

"Yes, I will. As soon as you like. After all, for the better part of a year, which is how long it's taken your line-breeding program to reach the fifth generation, we've been as good as engaged."

"We have?" said Charlie.

"That's how I thought of it, Charlie dear," said Merry. "I'd made up my mind to marry you long ago, but you wouldn't ask me. I told you once that you needed someone to help with the mice, and now that you've got this old giraffe to do, you'll need even more help. I like running the trains on the MMMR anyway, and I'll be able to keep an eye on this very special baby. I will

BRADFORD PUBLIC
LIBRARY DISTRICT

be much happier doing all that than going to a boring old office every day. So let's get married as soon as possible."

All this time Charlie had been on his knees, dumbstruck at how wonderful life had suddenly become.

Now he hoisted himself to his feet.

"Oh, Merry!" he said. "You have made me the happiest mouse farmer in the world!"

"And the happiest taxidermist?" said Merry.

"Yes!"

"Well, you'd better get back to work on that giraffe. I'll do the evening chores in here for you. That's if you'll trust me with the care of your green mouse?"

"*Our* green mouse," said Charlie. "He'd

never have been born if it hadn't been for all your encouragement and that idea of color-feeding."

"He ought to have a name, don't you think?" said Merry.

"Oh, yes. You choose one."

Merry thought for a moment.

"Well," she said, "Adam was the first man in the world. I don't know what color he was—not green, certainly—but just as certainly this is the first green buck mouse in the world. So how about 'Adam'? Or perhaps 'Adam Muffin'?"

"Great!" said Charlie. "We'll register him in that name with the National Mouse Club, because I'm determined about one thing, Merry. When he's old enough, we'll enter him in the Any Variety

Class at the Grand Mouse Championship Show. Just wait until all the other breeders first set eyes on Adam Muffin! How green they will be—with envy!"

Back in his workshop, Charlie whistled cheerily as he completed the fitting of the giraffe's forefoot. The tune he was whistling was the "Wedding March."

In the mouse shed, Merry sang merrily as she started and stopped the Dirty Train on its rounds and filled its little wagons with mucky bedding. The tune she was singing was "Charlie Is My Darling." When all her work was finished—all the mice freshly bedded, watered, and fed, the final locomotive (of the Food Train) parked in its shed beside its three companions, the cats, the owl, and Major all

switched on—she went into the workshop to say good-bye to Charlie.

The lower half of the giraffe, she found,
was now completed. The body stood
proudly in the center of the room on its
six-foot-long legs, the beautifully pat-
terned mottled hide stretched tight over
the wire frame within, the long tasseled
tail hanging down. All the creature lacked
was its neck and head.

Oh, I do hope he gets it all right,
thought Merry, because if the museum's
not satisfied, we'll have to keep the thing
here in the farmhouse, and the only way to
do that would be to stand it in the hall
with its neck sticking up the stairs.

"Good night, Charlie darling," she said.
"I must be going home now."

Charlie hugged her.

"Soon," he said, "you won't be going, because home will be here. How soon, d'you think?"

"Well," said Merry, "I've got to quit my job and you've got to finish your giraffe, and we've got all the arrangements for the wedding to make. So six weeks, say?"

"That'll be great," said Charlie, "because in just over six weeks it's the Grand Mouse Championship Show and Adam Muffin will be two months old. Tell you what, Merry, we'll go to London for our honeymoon, and we'll enter Adam in the Any Variety Class and we'll beat all of them. How about that?"

"Oh, Charlie," said Merry. "I do love you."

Chapter 8

Best in Show

Just over six weeks later, Mr. and Mrs. Charles Muffin were awoken very early by the sound of Mr. Muffin's budgie clock.

Clever do-it-yourself man that he was, he had converted an ordinary alarm clock into what he had intended to be a cuckoo clock. However, he was unable to lay his hands on a dead cuckoo, but he had been given a pet budgerigar—an Australian parakeet, that is—that had fallen off its perch, and he had stuffed that instead.

Now, at the hour of five o'clock, the budgie popped out of the mechanism, twittering and chattering loudly.

It was the day of the Grand Mouse Championship Show, a day when all the morning work in the mouse shed had to be done before they left for London. The evening work would have to wait till they returned.

Though each made great efforts to appear calm and unworried, both Charlie and Merry were tense and nervous. This was the day when all the top mouse fanciers would set their astonished eyes on Adam Muffin for the first time.

Their last job before they left the mouse shed was to groom him till his green coat shone. Then they put him into his carrying case with a little dry food and a slice of raw potato to provide moisture for him.

Merry carried the case into the farm-house, while Charlie switched on Major, and followed Merry, carrying Adam's grooming box and his show cage.

The grooming box was filled with soft hay, and on arrival at the show, Adam would be put into it to romp around and make himself spick-and-span before he was finally put into his show cage. This was a squarish container with a wire roof through which the judge could look down and see the mouse within.

Now Charlie and Merry waited for the

taxi that was to take them to the train station.

As they waited, Charlie took one last look around his workshop, which appeared amazingly empty, for by now the completed giraffe, head and neck joined at last to body, had gone to its final home in the Natural History Museum. It had traveled lying on its side on a large flatbed truck, and there were quite a few motorists who, suddenly seeing the fifteen-foot-tall figure, decided that they had better have their eyes checked.

Not only was the workshop empty, but the freezer held few bodies awaiting treatment—only a couple of hamsters and a corn snake—so that Charlie had no nagging worries about a backlog of work.

Then the taxi arrived, and Mr. and Mrs. Muffin set out on their one-day honeymoon.

Once at the show, Charlie took Adam Muffin from his carrying case and slipped him into his grooming box. His show cage stood ready in a long line of other show cages, each containing an entry for the Any Variety Class, but Charlie did not put him into it until the last possible moment, and then only when no one was looking. Finally, he covered the cage with a piece of cloth. Fellow mouse fanciers walked up and down, looking at the different exhibits.

"What have you got in there, then, Charlie?" someone said. "What's the idea, covering it up?"

"He's a bit nervous," Charlie said.

In fact, Adam wasn't the least bit nervous, but Charlie was, so much did he want this mouse to win, and Merry was, so much did she want Charlie to win.

When at last the judge came down the row of show cages and reached Charlie's, he said rather testily, "Now, come along, take off that cloth, please, this moment."

And Charlie whisked it off, and the astonished gaze of the judge fell upon Adam Muffin.

Adam stood, gazing up as though posing for a photographer. His well-groomed coat shone with health, his green coat green as a garden pea.

For a moment the judge was speechless. Then at last he found his voice.

"What in the world," he said croakily, "do you call this?"

"A green mouse," said Charlie Muffin.

Those nearest heard these words, and the news spread like wildfire throughout the great hall in which the show was being held.

"A *green* mouse! Someone's bred a *green* mouse!"

"Never!"

"That's what they're saying!"

"Where is it?"

"In the Any Variety Class. Come on, let's have a look!"

And it was not long before there was a great press of people, pushing and shoving in their eagerness to catch a glimpse of this extraordinary phenomenon.

For the rest of that unforgettable day at the Grand Mouse Championship Show, Charlie and Merry watched in a kind of trance as all their wildest dreams came true.

First, the judge (also in a kind of trance) made Adam Muffin the winner of the Any Variety Class. Then, when he had completed the judging of the other more usual color varieties, the time came for all the Class winners to compete against one another for the title of Best in Show.

As the judge moved slowly along the row of show cages containing the Class winners, the tension was unbearable. Everyone knew that one of those winners was the world's first-ever green mouse.

Everyone held their breath.

Charlie and Merry held hands tightly.

At last the judge turned to the watching throng.

He mopped his brow.

"The winner," he said in a hoarse voice, "of the Class for Best in Show, and therefore the Supreme Champion of the Grand Mouse Championship Show, is the green buck, Adam Muffin."

Chapter 9

Help Yourself, Burglar

By the time the triumphant trio had reached home and the evening round of cleaning and feeding had been done, Charlie Muffin and Merry Muffin were dog-tired and Adam Muffin was mouse-tired.

"He'd better have a cage to himself now," said Charlie. "He can go in this one, next door to your Antonia and Cleopatra."

"And I suppose you'll pin that big red rosette marked CHAMPION on the front?" said Merry.

"Yes, of course. Why not?"

"You might just as well hang a sign beside it saying HERE HE IS. HELP YOUR-SELF, BURGLAR."

"Not much point in anyone stealing him," said Charlie. "Everyone knows that ours is the only green mouse in the world. No one could ever show him."

"No, but they could use him for breed-ing," said Merry.

"Which is what *we* want him for," said Charlie. "You're right. Tell you what. We'll put him back in his carrying case and he can sleep under our bed tonight. Tomor-row I'll think of a way to keep him safe."

Charlie was as good as his word. His plan was simple. He went to town and bought two bottles of vegetable dyes, which, he made sure, were soluble and would not harm the skin. One bottle contained green dye, one black.

First, he took a white buck mouse (black-eyed, as Adam was) and very carefully, with Merry's help, he dyed it green and stuck the red rosette on the front of its cage.

Then, even more carefully, he dyed Adam black.

"That ought to do it!" he said to Merry. "I almost wish a burglar would come, just for the fun of it."

Some weeks later, his wish came true.

In the middle of the night, Major began

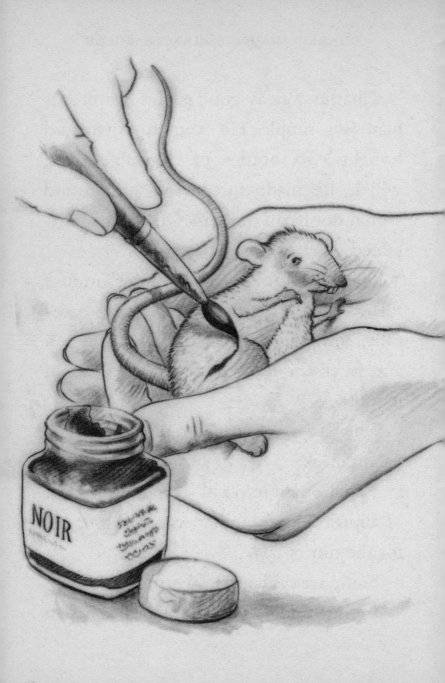

to bark and growl, and Charlie jumped out of bed and rushed down to the control panel in the workshop to send the usual warning message over the intercom. But by the time he reached the mouse shed, the lock of whose door had been picked, the intruder had fled.

Hastily, while the dog barked and the cats meowed and the owl hooted, Charlie opened Adam's cage.

There he sat, black as night but safe and sound.

But the door of the cage on which the red rosette was pinned hung open. The once-white, now green-dyed, buck was gone.

"Trouble is," said Charlie at breakfast the next morning, "we'll have to keep on dyeing white mice green in case of more burglaries."

"Wait a minute," said Merry. "I've got a better idea. There's only one sure reason why no one would ever again try to steal Adam."

"And what's that?"

"If he'd *already* been stolen."

"Well, he hasn't been."

"You know that and I know that, but the fact remains that last night someone stole a green mouse from you, didn't they?"

"Yes, but..."

"Tell the world!" said Merry. "Tell the local newspaper and write to whatever magazine it is that mouse farmers read—"

"The *Mouse Breeders' Gazette*."

"—and let them know about the theft."

"Merry," said Charlie, "you are brilliant!"

So it came about that not only the local paper but several of the national dailies ran a story about the man who, "after a lifetime of endeavor," had bred the only green mouse ever seen, only to have it stolen.

The *Mouse Breeders' Gazette* was almost lyrical in the depth of its regret:

SUPREME CHAMPION STOLEN

Fellow mouse fanciers will join with us in offering our deepest sympathy to Mr. and Mrs. Charles Muffin on their sad loss. Adam Muffin, Supreme Champion at the Grand Mouse

Championship Show, and the first and only green mouse in the world, was stolen from the Muffins' mouse shed, an act of wanton wickedness which we all deplore. One thing is certain—namely, that the thief will never dare exhibit this animal in any show ring.

"Or if he does," said Merry, "we'll be there with a wet sponge to show him what color his green mouse really is!"

"And when he breeds from it," said Charlie, "he's in for a bit of a disappointment! We're the only ones with a chance of breeding more green mice."

Which is something that, over the

coming months, Charlie worked hard on. The notebook filled up with details of the many greenish-blue does in the line-breeding program who were mated with Adam Muffin in the hope of reproducing that pea-green color that lay beneath his black-dyed coat.

At about ten days of age, each new litter of cubs was eagerly examined by the Muffins, but each time without success. By the time Charlie and Merry Muffin celebrated their first wedding anniversary, Adam Muffin, now restored to his original color, had fathered hundreds and hundreds of babies. But never was there a green cub among them.

"D'you think we'll ever breed another?" Charlie asked.

"I can't say," replied Merry.

Charlie grinned.

"There's no such word as *can't*," he said. "Though I expect your old aunt would have something to say about this whole business."

"She would, Charlie dear," said Merry. "She'd say, 'Count your blessings,'" and she smiled at him.

"How right she'd be," said Charlie. "I've got you, that's the greatest blessing, and I've got Adam, and the other mice are selling well, and the freezer is pretty full of animals (including one of ours, incidentally, an old chocolate doe from cage 62. I must prepare her tomorrow—she'll look nice on the mantelpiece)."

"You forgot something else that's on the mantelpiece," said Merry, and she pointed at the little silver cup, the National Mouse Club's highest award.

"*You* won that," she said.

"*We* won that," said Charlie.

"*Adam* won that," they said with one voice.

"So even if you never succeed in breeding another green mouse, Charlie," said Merry, "you'll always have the memory of that triumph. By the way, since we're talking about counting blessings, there's another one still to come."

"Oh?" said Charlie. "What's that?"

"I'm going to have a baby."

Chapter 10

Cherry

Suggesting a name for the coming baby was something on which Charlie and Merry spent a good deal of time. They thought of lots of boys' names and lots of girls' names, but they couldn't agree on a single one.

"It'd be a lot easier," Charlie said, "if only we knew which it was going to be."

"I'm sure it's a girl," said Merry.

"How can you be sure?"

"I just am."

"Tell you what," Charlie said, "I've got an idea. Your old aunt may have lots of sayings, but my old grandfather had a party trick that he did a good few times, and it always came out right. My mother told me he tried it on her when she was pregnant with me, and the ring said it was a boy and I was."

"The ring? Whatever do you mean?" Merry said.

"Well, I remember my mother telling me how it worked. First she had to pull a long hair from her head and then take off her wedding ring and thread the long hair through it. Then my grandfather held the ends of the strand and dangled the ring over my mother's tummy. 'If the ring circles around and around,' my grand-father said to her, 'you're carrying a girl. If it swings to and fro like a pendulum, it's a boy.'"

"What fun!" said Merry.

She pulled out a long strand of hair and threaded it through her wedding ring.

"Try it, Charlie," she said.

So Charlie tried it, and the ring began to go around and around in circles.

"I told you!" Merry said. "I knew it was a girl. Now we can concentrate on a name for a girl—so how about Charlotte?"

"Why Charlotte?" asked Charlie.

"It's got the first five letters of your name," said Merry.

"No, that's no good," said her husband. "She'd only get to be called Charlie for short, and then there'd be two of us. I've got a better idea. Let's use the first two letters of my name and the last four of yours. Cherry! Cherry Muffin—how does that sound?" said Charlie.

"It sounds lovely," said his wife. "Cherry it is!"

And Cherry it was. Some months later, her birth was announced not only in the local newspaper but also in the *Mouse Breeders' Gazette* and the *Taxidermists' Chronicle*.

So time passed happily at the mouse farm, till Cherry grew old enough to be carried around the mouse shed and shown Major and the cats and the owl and the

MMMR at work, and to see all the different colors of mice.

Best of all, she liked one particular mouse, and before long she spoke her first word, which sounded remarkably like "Adam."

Thankfully, she was too young to realize that, even in the happiest of lives, there is sadness, nor could she possibly know that the life of a pet mouse is not a very long one.

One morning Charlie and Merry were taking their daughter around the shed, and as they approached the green mouse's cage, Cherry began to call out, "Adam! Adam!"

But when they reached the cage, it was empty.

"Where Adam?" said Cherry.

"He's gone away," said her father.

"She'll miss him, won't she?" said Merry that evening.

"No, she won't," said Charlie. "We'll soon see him again."

And so they did, for before long a new figure stood in the middle of the Muffins' mantelpiece, a figure mounted proudly upon a little pedestal on which was fixed a brass plaque, which read:

ADAM MUFFIN
SUPREME CHAMPION

Then they lifted Cherry up and said to her, "Who's that?"

"Adam!" she cried. "Nice Adam!" and happily she stroked his pea-green back.

"Bless her!" said Merry. "She thinks he's still alive."

"Dear old chap," said Charlie. "It's lovely to think that now Cherry will always remember our miracle mouse."

ABOUT THE AUTHOR

DICK KING-SMITH was born and raised in Gloucestershire, England. After twenty years as a farmer, he turned to teaching and then to writing the children's books that have earned him critical acclaim on both sides of the Atlantic. Mr. King-Smith is the author of numerous books for children, including *The Roundhill*, *Mr. Ape*, *A Mouse Called Wolf*, and *Babe: The Gallant Pig*, which was made into an award-winning major motion picture.